Australia is a rugged nation. It is home for people from countries all over the world. Each one is an Australian, no matter where their families came from.

They are a people famous for their good sportsmanship and love of a good time. But as in so many other melting-pot countries, Australia has its problems with race differences.

This is a story about the Way to solve such problems. Sandy tries to say if we are all "rescued" then we all become equal.

SANDY
THE GIRL WHO WAS RESCUED
by Douglas Blackwood
Photos by Douglas Blackwood
© Copyright 1987 by Scandinavia
Publishing House, Nørregade 32, DK1165 Copenhagen K.
English-language edition first published 1988
through special arrangement with Scandinavia
jointly by Wm.B. Eerdmans Publishing Co.,
255 Jefferson Ave. S.E., Grand Rapids, Michigan 49503

Printed in Hong Kong

ISBN 0-8028-5026-X

SANDY
The Girl Who Was Rescued

Douglas Blackwood

Photos by Douglas Blackwood

962

William B. Eerdmans Publishing Company
Grand Rapids, Michigan

Sandy was in big trouble. A huge wave crashed down on her surfboard. She just could not hold on anymore. The wave flipped the surfboard over as if it were a feather and bounced it all the way to the beach. Sandy was pulled underneath the white water. Almost out of breath, she struggled to the surface. Smash! No sooner had she gulped some air than another wave swept over her.

Sandy wished she had never gone out in such big waves. She knew better. Why, she barely knew how to stand up on the surfboard. It had been a birthday gift from her parents when she turned ten last month.

Earlier that same morning, Sandy had gone to the beach with her friends, Suzanne and Jenny. Her house in Sydney, Australia's largest city, looked out over the beach. She could see the waves from her window. At night Sandy fell asleep to the sound of the surf breaking on the shore. She loved the waves.

It was a very hot January day, just perfect for the beach. Summer was at Christmas time because Australia was south of the Equator. That day, when Sandy had run across the scorching hot sand into the water, she had thought only of fun. Danger never even entered her mind. And yet...

"Help me! Hel...!" Sandy screamed as another wave crashed on top of her, tumbling her over and over until her lungs felt like they would burst. A sharp cramp shot up her leg. The pain was terrible. With her last bit of strength she fought her way up to the surface. She swallowed a mouthful of air and water. "Help," she called out again. Her voice could not be heard because the waves were too loud. She looked up and saw the open sea. A strong **rip current** pulled Sandy outward, away from the shore. The sky began to spin. Sandy was close to drowning.

Suzanne and Jenny had noticed Sandy's surfboard washed onto the beach. But they could not see Sandy anywhere and were worried.

At that same time, two **lifesavers** keeping watch at the other end of the beach saw Sandy in trouble.

"Greg, look!" one of them called out. "Look out past the waves breaking! Do you see someone?"

"Let's go! I'll take the rescue board!" said Greg. The two lifesavers sprinted into the water.

They were two of hundreds of volunteer lifesavers patrolling the twentysix ocean beaches along Sydney's coastline. Every time they helped rescue someone from drowning, they risked their own lives.

Greg paddled his rescue board out between the roaring waves. When a large wave approached, he rolled under the board just before it broke over the top. They reached Sandy just in time. She could hardly stay afloat.

"Hold onto my board!" Greg yelled out, getting a mouthful of water as a wave washed by.

"I can't move. I've a cramp in my leg!" cried Sandy. The other lifesaver swam behind Sandy and pushed her onto the board. A wave twisted the board around sharply. Greg slipped off and the edge of the board smashed into his head. Frantically, he climbed back on.

"Lie down flat!" Greg shouted to Sandy. "Let's get out'a here! Quickly!" His head ached. Waiting for just the right moment, he paddled as fast as he could. Suddenly, the swell picked up the board, pushing it forward. "Thank you!" he called out as the board glided down the face of a wave.

Sandy, lying on the front end, wondered for a split second whom Greg was thanking. But the thrill of the ride distracted her. She felt a rush of excitement as the water raced beneath her. Nothing, not even danger, she decided, would stop her from wanting to surf again.

The two lifesavers staggered up the beach, carrying Sandy between them.

"You can put me down!" she said, embarrassed by all the staring people.

"Are you sure you're O.K.?" asked Greg.

"Of course I'm all right," she yelled back.

Greg let Sandy down and she sat on the beach, trying to catch her breath. The other lifesaver went back to the lookout to keep watch. Greg rubbed his head. "I got a thump by the board."

Sandy suddenly realized how selfish she had been. "Are you hurt?" she asked meekly.

"I'll live," joked Greg. "Don't feel bad about being rescued. I was rescued once...by a school of dolphin!"

"You're kidding me, aren't you?" asked Sandy.

"I'm not. I was out surfing alone when a huge shark circled me. I was scared out of my mind. Then a school of dolphin suddenly appeared. They darted around, pushing the shark, and finally drove it away. I'm sure it was God watching over me."

"Do you believe in God?" asked Sandy, now realizing who it was Greg had thanked out on the wave. She knew she didn't believe in God.

"Since then, I do," said Greg. "I believe he watches over all of us."

Sandy felt awkward talking about God. She changed the subject. "Do you ride a surfboard?"

"Sure," said Greg modestly. He was actually a champion surfer. "Next weekend I'm driving up the coast to surf some deserted beaches with a few **mates.**"

Sandy's eyes got big. The best waves of all were to be found up the coast. "Can I come too?"

"I don't know.... I mean you are...a bit young," muttered Greg.

"I'm not that young!" snapped Sandy. "Anyway, I could come with my older brother. He's a surfer. And my friend Suzanne, she loves to surf."

Greg laughed. "All right, I'll ask the others."

"Great!" declared Sandy. Then she saw Suzanne and Jenny coming up the beach. "I've got to go," she said, getting up stiffly.

"Hey, what's your name?" asked Greg.

"Sandy," she shouted back as she hobbled off. Greg sat, rubbing his head and smiling to himself.

At home Sandy did not tell her parents everything that happened. She did not want them to know how foolish she had been to go out into the rough waves. Instead, she asked over and over again if she could please go on the surfing trip. They finally said "yes", but only if her older brother Mark went along, too. Sandy dragged Mark into her bedroom and would not let him leave until he had said "yes." She was also able to convince Suzanne. Her friend liked the idea of surfing on deserted beaches. Greg's friends grumbled when they first heard about the girls coming along. They only agreed when Greg said, "The girls can at least stand up on their surfboards." Sandy was a little bit angry when she heard Greg and his friends were making jokes about her.

The night before they left, Sandy dug out her old sleeping bag from where she'd stored it for months. It smelled of mothballs. The plan was to leave before sunrise — they had such a long way to go.

When Greg arrived in his old van to pick up Sandy and Mark, she had not yet finished breakfast. Then, because she could not find her purse, they had to wait another hour.

They drove north until the middle of the afternoon. Then Greg pulled into a small beach at the end of a long, dirt road. The others were waiting for them. Greg and Mark teased Sandy about having made them late. She pouted and would not smile the whole time they were putting up the tents. She could not stand to be teased.

When the camp was set up, they decided there was still enough light for them to go surfing off the point. "Sorry, Sandy, but you had better not come in today. The surf is a bit too wild for you." Sandy's brother agreed. She felt like she wanted to scream, she was so mad. And because Suzanne was a better surfer and could go with the others, Sandy felt even worse. She wished she had never come.

From where Sandy sat, she could see Suzanne and the others catching the waves off the point. The water sparkled in the sun. For a moment she thought about why so many surfers say they find God while on the waves. The waves help you think. But then Sandy went back to feeling sorry for herself.

11

At the far end of the deserted beach Sandy saw some oddly shaped rocks weathered by the sea. She wandered down to them and climbed the sandstone figures. Some of them looked like strange faces. A breeze whistled through the rocks. Sandy thought the place felt spooky. At the top of the cliff was a thick line of eucalyptus trees. She decided to do some exploring. The undergrowth was sharp and scratched her legs. She found a narrow path formed by wild rabbits. It led up the hill away from the beach. A kangaroo hopped through the bush ahead of her. Sandy hurried to get a closer look. She climbed a big rock, but the kangaroo had disappeared.

Suddenly, out of the corner of her eye, Sandy saw someone watching her. She froze. A tall Aborigine, a native Australian, stood opposite her. Neither moved for what seemed a long time. Sandy wanted to run away, but her legs felt like lead weights. The Aborigine took a step towards Sandy. She screamed, and he stepped quickly backwards. Sandy turned around and slid down the rock face. She heard the man call out, "Don't go!" His voice was soft and gentle. Sandy looked back at the man. He grinned, and the features on his sun-blackened face cracked and fell into wrinkles.

"Don't be afraid," he said kindly. "My name is Walloo Walloo. I belong to an Aborigine tribe which lives nearby." He stooped down, picked a bright wild-flower, and offered it to Sandy. "Here, take this; it's called a honey flower. It's sweet."

Sandy reached out cautiously, took the flower from Walloo Walloo, and sniffed it. Her hand was shaking. She had never seen a tribal Aborigine before. She knew that many tribes lived in special settlements, but had not known there was one nearby.

13

"**Are** you lost?" asked Walloo Walloo.

"No," replied Sandy bravely, but she still trembled a little. "My friends are surfing. They won't let me surf because I had to be rescued once."

"Rescued!" exclaimed Walloo Walloo. "An Aborigine thinks it's a great honor to be rescued. Every year my tribe celebrates the day it was rescued from a big **bush** fire. Flames surrounded our camp, but a little dog showed us the way out."

"A little dog!" exclaimed Sandy, but she hesitated. The way the man looked made her uncomfortable. She had thought Aborigines were primitives.

"Do you see the giant kangaroo carved on the rock?" Sandy could hardly see the ancient carving in the rock, it was so well worn. So Walloo Walloo outlined it with stones. Sandy helped him, then sat on the rock as Walloo Walloo told her a story.

"In the Dreamtime lived Bahomi, the water spirit. Bahomi was grieved because some men had caught Biami, the golden fish who made every morning glow. From that day the sunrise lost its golden glow. Changra, the giant kangaroo, came to the sea in search for Biami. He looked over the whole land and finally found Biami locked in a **billabong**, a waterhole, which glowed gold. Changra offered himself in exchange for Biami. The men were so glad to catch a giant kangaroo they agreed. So Changra was captured and Biami returned to the sea. And that's how gold came back to the dawn."

"What a sad story," said Sandy.

"Yes, but each golden dawn also gives great hope," said Walloo Walloo. Sandy listened as he told another story.

Walloo Walloo told many stories that afternoon until the shadows had grown quite long and Sandy realized she should go back to the camp. As she climbed down the slope to the beach, she waved, knowing she would probably never see Walloo Walloo again.

Early the next morning Sandy went back to the rock with Suzanne and Greg. They waited, hoping to see Walloo Walloo. The air was very hot and still. No one spoke; only the **cicada** drummed loudly. The kangaroo on the rock looked more worn and ancient. Several hours passed. Sandy finally decided to go back to the beach with her friends. Walloo Walloo had become like a dream.

At the end of January the summer vacation was over. In Sandy's class all the students had to describe what they had done during their time away from school. Sandy told about Walloo Walloo and held up a **nullanulla**. The Aboriginal wooden club, which he had given to her, was decorated with painted kangaroos and snakes. A boy at the back of the class started to giggle. Sandy glared at him. "What's so funny?" she asked.

"Abos are **boongs**," spat the boy. A boong was a bad name for Aborigines. "They eat **witchetty grubs** out of the ground. Yuk!"

"Walloo Walloo is not a boong!" snapped Sandy.

"Walloo Walloo, Walloo," teased several of the boys. The class burst out laughing.

"That's enough," said the teacher. Sandy turned bright red and ran to her seat, almost in tears.

Just then, the bell rang for the end of the lesson. The class packed up and there was a rush for the door. Sandy did not move. She hated the boys, though she realized that once she would have laughed the same way.

"Come on, Sandy!" called out Jenny. "Don't let those silly boys get to you. We'll go and talk to Mrs. Andrews."

Mrs. Andrews taught a special class called "Scripture." In Australia, the public schools have one class about the Bible a week. Mrs. Andrews was in the playground, and Sandy told her all about what had happened. She listened understandingly. "I have an idea," she said. "I'll see what I can do."

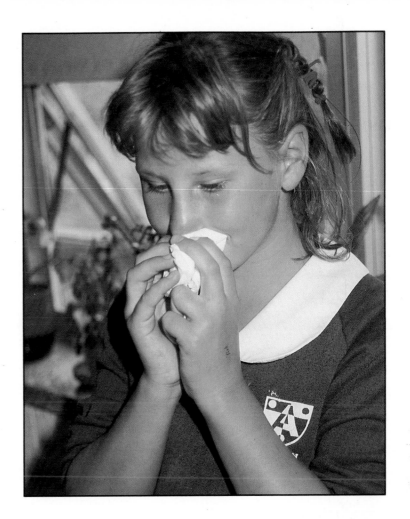

Several days later Mrs. Andrews phoned Sandy. "Are you free Saturday? I want you and Jenny to meet some friends of mine. They are Aborigines living in the city. We'll go by ferryboat."

When Saturday came, Sandy and Jenny showed up with Suzanne and another friend, Peter. They all squashed into Mrs. Andrews' tiny car. The trip across Sydney Harbor was beautiful. Sailing boats covered the water.

Sandy leaned over the side and watched the water break against the bow. She was lost in her thoughts. Mrs. Andrews saw her and smiled. "Thinking?" she asked.

Sandy looked up. "Why doesn't my class like Walloo Walloo?" she asked.

"They don't know him like you do," said Mrs. Andrews. "And because he is different, they don't understand his ways. God, though, understands us all, and loves us as different as we are."

"But God only loves good people, doesn't He?" asked Sandy.

"He loves every person the same," said Mrs. Andrews. "And He also loves what's good for us."

The ferry was about to pull into the city wharf. Thick ropes were thrown out to hold the boat. Sandy stared at the surge of water swirling around the wharf. She thought about how she sometimes said things she did not mean. She wondered if God could love her, too. The gangplank was lowered. A crowd of people going to the beach stood on the wharf, waiting to go the other way. Some carried surfboards under their arms. Sandy realized she was missing out on a perfect surfing day. But she also felt she was beginning a much bigger adventure.

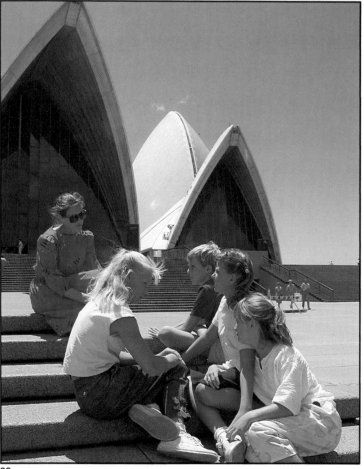

Near the wharf was the Sydney Opera House. Its enormous, white-tiled roof glistened in the sun. "Can we visit the opera house first?" shouted Peter. And before Mrs. Andrews could reply, he ran off, followed by the three girls. An enormous flight of steps led up to the podium. By the time Mrs. Andrews had reached the top, the children were mischievously sliding on a sloping piece of roof.

"I want you to count how many steps you ran up," she asked, catching her breath. The four raced to the bottom, then started slowly up again.

"Seventy-two!" they all agreed, puffing heavily.

"Now tell me," said Mrs. Andrews. "How long ago did the first settlers come to Sydney?"

Suzanne knew the answer, "200 years."

"That's right. The first white Australians were convicts sent from English prisons," said Mrs. Andrews. "Now I want you to run up 200 steps." Peter raced back down and the girls reluctantly followed. They had to go up and down almost three times before they covered 200 steps. Finally, they were panting and had to sit down.

Mrs. Andrews chuckled. "The next question is: How long have the Aborigines been in Australia?" None of them knew. "What if I told you well over 40,000 years?"

"Oh no!" cried out Peter. "I'm not going to run up 40,000 steps!"

"Anyone else want to try?" teased Mrs. Andrews. They all shook their heads. "I think we all need to have much more respect for the Aboriginal people."

"Mrs. Andrews, where do the Aborigines live that you know?" asked Sandy.

"Let's take the train to meet them; then you can see for yourselves," replied Mrs. Andrews. She got up from the steps. The others followed, dragging their tired feet.

The train took them to a very run-down place. They had to step over broken glass and bricks. Some Aborigines sat on the sidewalk curb. Sandy did not like the way they stared at her. Then out of one doorway came a smiling couple and three children.

"**G'day**, Mrs. Andrews," the man said. "I'm glad you came."

"This is Pastor Jack," said Mrs. Andrews. "And Pearl, and Ben and Marvina. She is almost the same age as you, Sandy." Sandy looked shyly at Marvina, who reached out to shake her hand. Sandy thought of Walloo Walloo offering the flower. But Marvina was very different, more like herself.

"Ya' wanna play cricket?" chirped Ben.

"That's a good idea," said Pastor Jack. "Mom and I will talk to Mrs. Andrews inside."

Sandy had often played cricket at school. The rules for playing street cricket were much simpler, though. Whoever either caught or bowled out the batter got to bat next. Sandy was asked to bat first. Ben bowled her out on the first ball. From then on Ben did all the batting. He was an expert at street cricket. Sandy and her friends felt left out. After some time Ben mishit a ball high into the air and Sandy was sure she was going to catch it. But the moment before the ball landed in her outstretched fingers, Marvina leaped a fraction higher and snatched it away. "You're out, Ben!" she shouted.

Sandy glared at Marvina. "That was going to be my catch."

"Go on, you can bat, Sandy," said Marvina. Sandy realized her selfishness, though, and turned down the offer.

"Someone has got to bat!" yelled Ben. So Sandy took up the bat. This time she surprized everyone with her batting. Eventually she passed Ben's high score.

"We'll never get her out," Ben complained. Marvina giggled at her brother.

After a while, Sandy announced, "I want Marvina to bat in my place!"

"Thanks, **mate**," said Marvina, winking. "My brothers won't have a chance against us." The two girls batted on for over an hour, swapping places. The action attracted a small crowd of onlookers.

Pearl came outside with a tray of drinks. "I hope you are getting on fine," she said.

"Marvina and Sandy are!" exclaimed Ben.

"There's a train to catch," reminded Pearl. "So drink up."

Once the lemonade was gulped down they all walked to the station. Sandy and Marvina talked the whole way. "My Dad used to work on a cattle ranch," said Marvina. "Then he became a pastor and came here."

"What's it like having a pastor for a Dad?" asked Sandy.

"It's **beaut!**" replied Marvina. "We often go **outback**. Then we pray under the stars, and God becomes big, really big." The outback was the vast wilderness in the middle of Australia.

Sandy had never been to the outback, but still understood. "The stars over the ocean are like that."

The train was late. Everyone was glad to have the extra time together. Jenny and Sandy braided Marvina's long, thick black hair.

"Can I visit your house?" Marvina asked Sandy.

"You can go surfing with me! I'll teach you," shouted Sandy as the train rattled into the station. Mrs. Andrews shook hands with Pastor Jack and Pearl. Marvina hugged Sandy very tight.

"I'm glad I came," said Sandy, stepping onto the train. "Come as soon as you can, Marvina," she called out as the train doors slid shut. The train lurched forward and picked up speed. Sandy waved as Marvina and her family disappeared from view.

In the weeks which followed, the two girls called each other almost every day. Pearl then suggested they write instead. "The phone bill is getting high."

In her first letter Sandy wrote, "...and guess what project we had to do in class? Aborigines! Everyone thought I was the expert. Don't tell, but I just made up answers off the top of my head. There are no Aborigines at my school, so no one knew the difference. Then I felt bad, so my girlfriends helped me look up 'Aborigines' in the school library.... Did you know there are hundreds of Aboriginal languages? Why do you speak only English? It's my worst subject...."

Marvina wrote back to Sandy, "...English is my favorite subject. My Dad can speak his tribal language, but he says we need English.... My school is a mixture of kids from lots of places, like Italy, Greece, and Vietnam. But my teacher is an **Aussie**.... Yesterday, when I bought an ice cream at the store, I saw a big fight in the street. A bus load of police came and people were throwing bottles and bricks and yelling things against the 'boongs'. I get so scared and want to move when that happens. But we need to stay to help...."

Sandy answered back, "...I saw news of the fighting on T.V. I can't believe you were there, too. I was worried when I read your letter. Sometimes it seems like you are in a different country.... We had our school swimming races. I was in the class relay. We won! Mom hugged me afterwards. I felt like a hero...."

Marvina wrote back, "...You must be a great swimmer. Our swimming races were called off because the pool has been closed all summer.... Mom says I can visit you for Easter. That's only two weeks away. Wow, then we can surf together.... I'm praying for you. Your best mate, Marvina."

On Good Friday Marvina's father drove her across Sydney to visit Sandy. It was a long drive. Once out of the big city, Marvina was amazed by the many golden beaches and rocky cliffs they passed. Where she lived, she never saw the sea. Sandy's street twisted around one of the headlands. They were late by the time they found the right street. Marvina saw Sandy waving at them.

"We got lost," explained Marvina, leaning out of the car window. Then her eyes rivetted onto Sandy's house, which was perched on a cliff overlooking the ocean. "Is this really your house? It's like a palace!"

"Have a good time and behave yourself," said Marvina's father. She jumped out of the car and waved as her father drove off. She followed Sandy down some steps to the house.

"Are you hungry?" asked Sandy.

"I'm starving. What have you got?" said Marvina. When they went into the kitchen she gaped at all the modern, shiny appliances.

Marvina met Sandy's mother, who said, "Make yourself at home." So she did, and she wandered from room to room, then onto the deck which stuck out from the house and over the beach. She peered over the edge. "I feel like a bird up here," she said happily, looking down at the waves.

"Once, I almost drowned in the surf," said Sandy, recalling how desperate she had been. "The waves were very fierce. Two lifesavers swam out and rescued me."

"You were rescued! I thought you were a good swimmer," teased Marvina.

"I wasn't good enough," admitted Sandy. "Come on, I'll take you down to the beach and show you where it happened."

The girls climbed down a steep path. The hot sand crunched under their feet. They let the cool water swirl around their ankles. Sandy pointed to where she had been dragged out to sea.

"I felt very stupid when I was rescued," she said, remembering how she had first reacted with Greg. Now, they often went surfing together. Greg had become a leader at the surf club. "But later," she continued, "a wonderful, old Aborigine taught me it is an honor to be rescued. Have you ever been rescued?"

"Yes, but not in the surf," replied Marvina.

"Where?" asked Sandy, curiously.

"Nowhere," said Marvina, smiling secretly.

"But you were rescued?"

"Sure," said Marvina. "Jesus rescued me. He lost His life saving mine."

"You mean Jesus is like a lifesaver?" asked Sandy.

"Yes, except He can save all of us, if we call out to Him."

"Like in a mass rescue," said Sandy, realizing something more. "There was a mass rescue here a month ago. An underwater sandbank collapsed and over twenty swimmers standing on it were washed out to sea. They all needed to be rescued. It didn't matter if they were good or bad swimmers!" Sandy paused to think for a moment. Then she added softly, "And it didn't matter what color skin they had."

Marvina flashed a grin at her friend.

The pieces were falling together for Sandy. She understood how she and Marvina could both be rescued by Jesus. It didn't matter what their background. They were equal.

Sandy gazed out to sea. A lone surfer was on the waves. Was it Greg? The wind blew her hair back off her face. Yes, it was true, she thought. God does speak on the waves.

"Come on, Marvina," she said. "Let's go back and get my surfboard. I'm going to teach you how to surf. And you can teach me how to talk to God, on the waves."

"For he has rescued us from the dominion of darkness and brought us into the kingdom of the Son he loves, in whom we have redemption, the forgiveness of sins."

Colossians 1:13-14 NIV

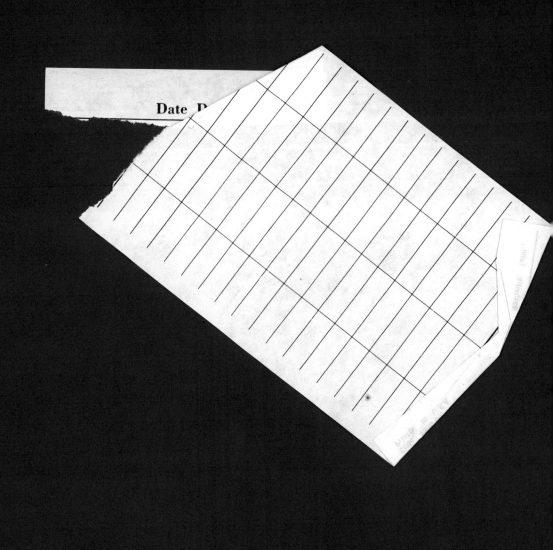

Date D